Wonders of the Arctic

By Elsie Nelley

Contents

How the Northern Lights Occur

The northern lights glow as a blaze of colour in the night sky around the Arctic Circle.

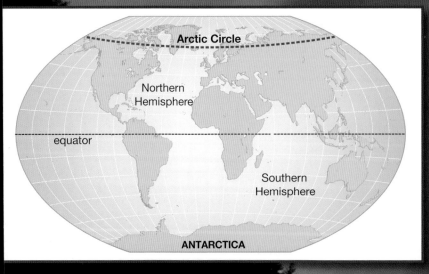

They occur most often from September to April and are only visible within the Northern Hemisphere. The lights are caused by particles that come from the Sun's surface.

The surface of the Sun is not a quiet place. Storms and giant explosions occur there. When these happen, millions of tiny particles that contain electricity, break away from the surface of the Sun. The particles are thrown out into space and carried away from the Sun by the solar wind. The solar wind flows towards and around the planets, including Earth, in space.

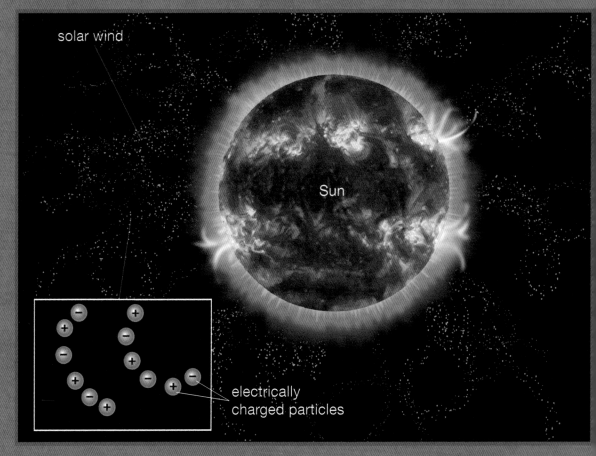

solar wind

Sun

electrically
charged particles

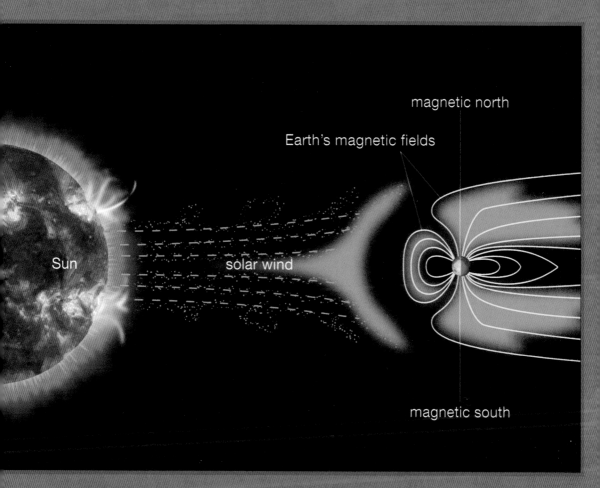

magnetic north

Earth's magnetic fields

Sun

solar wind

magnetic south

In space, Earth acts like a huge magnet. Some particles become trapped in Earth's magnetic fields when the solar wind blows in the direction of Earth. The trapped particles are then pulled downwards by Earth's two magnetic poles.

When these particles meet with gases in the sky far above Earth, energy is released. Some of the energy glows and appears as coloured lights in the sky. Different gases produce different colours.

The most common colour produced by the gases is green. However, shades of red, blue and purple are also seen. Sometimes, the colours are so pale they can hardly be seen at all. At other times they can be extremely bright. When the solar wind blows strongly, the colour of the lights is more spectacular.

The northern lights appear in several shapes. They can often be seen as a curve of light that shimmers up and down, filling the sky with colour. From time to time, they appear as smooth bands of coloured light stretching up towards the night sky. Sometimes the northern lights are visible as wide bands of wavy colour that constantly change from bright to dim and back again.

the southern lights

The lights that are seen around the Arctic Circle are called *aurora borealis*. Similar lights appear in southern regions around Antarctica and are called the southern lights or *aurora australis*.

Saturday, 20 March at 5.30 p.m.

The Iditarod Sled Dog Race

Recently, Dad and I travelled to Anchorage, Alaska, for the start of the Iditarod Trail Race. Although we arrived really early, thousands of noisy, enthusiastic spectators had already jostled for the best places behind the barriers erected on either side of the street. Television cameras whirred and instructions bellowed from loudspeakers, amidst the hustle and bustle of the 90 teams making last-minute preparations.

Officials also rushed around checking that the mushers had essential equipment and food safely packed on their sleds. Volunteers with clipboards verified the tags on each dog. Then, they checked that the boots worn by the dogs to protect their feet against cutting ice and hard, packed snow had been securely fastened.

As the start time ticked down towards ten o'clock, the noise slowly changed to a hush. First, a short ribbon-cutting ceremony was held beside the flags representing the home countries and states of all the competitors.

Then, at exactly ten o'clock, the first musher and his dogs departed along the snow-covered street. The thousands of spectators who had travelled to see this momentous event clapped and cheered. The race had finally begun!

Next, the remaining mushers and their teams of 12 to 16 dogs followed; each separated by two-minute intervals. Many of the dogs had to be restrained on leads as they eagerly anticipated their turn. The huge, cheering crowd shouted encouragement to every team as the competitors set out on their challenging journey.

During this unique race, the courageous mushers and their dogs travelled over a trail of jagged mountain ranges, frozen rivers, dense forests and windswept coasts.

Their journey was made even more hazardous by sub-zero temperatures, gale-force winds and long hours of darkness.

It took the mushers and their dogs between eight to 15 days to reach the finishing post, where they were all greeted as heroes. Now I understand why this race is often called the "Last Great Race on Earth".